Sports Illustrated KIDS

GOODNIGHT

BY **MICHAEL DAHL**

ILLUSTRATED BY **CHRISTINA FORSHAY**

PICTURE WINDOW BOOKS
A CAPSTONE IMPRINT

The great big stadium is outside of town.

Fans and friends come
from miles around.

We walk through the gates.

We each take our places . . .

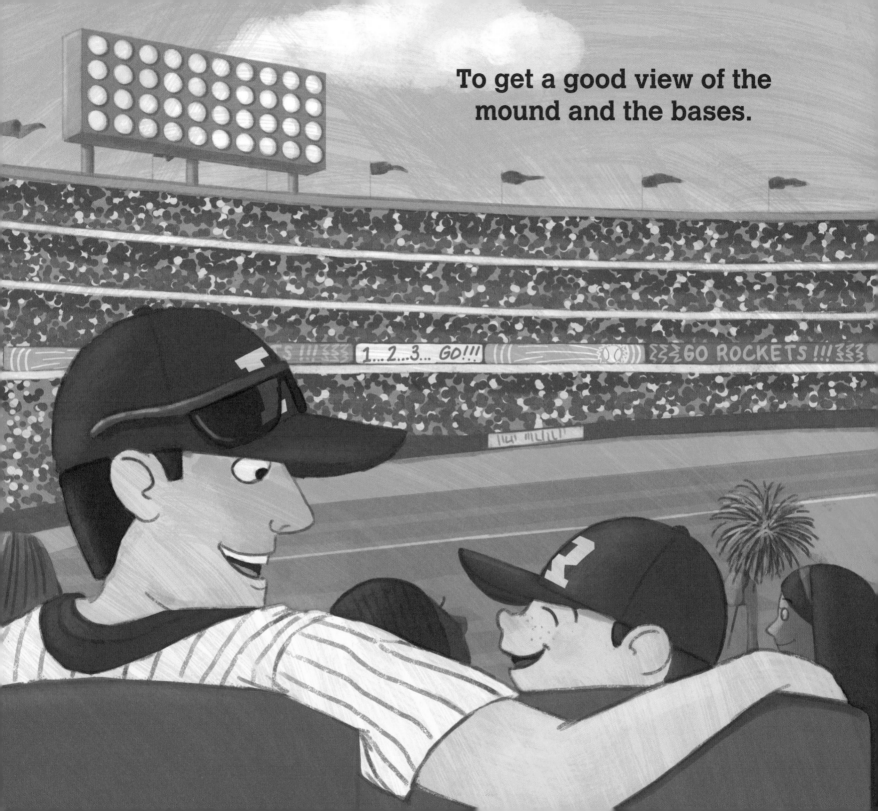

To get a good view of the
mound and the bases.

We eat popcorn and hot dogs
and hold drinks in our laps . . .

with the names of
our favorite teams
bright on our caps.

We watch all the players
who catch and who throw,

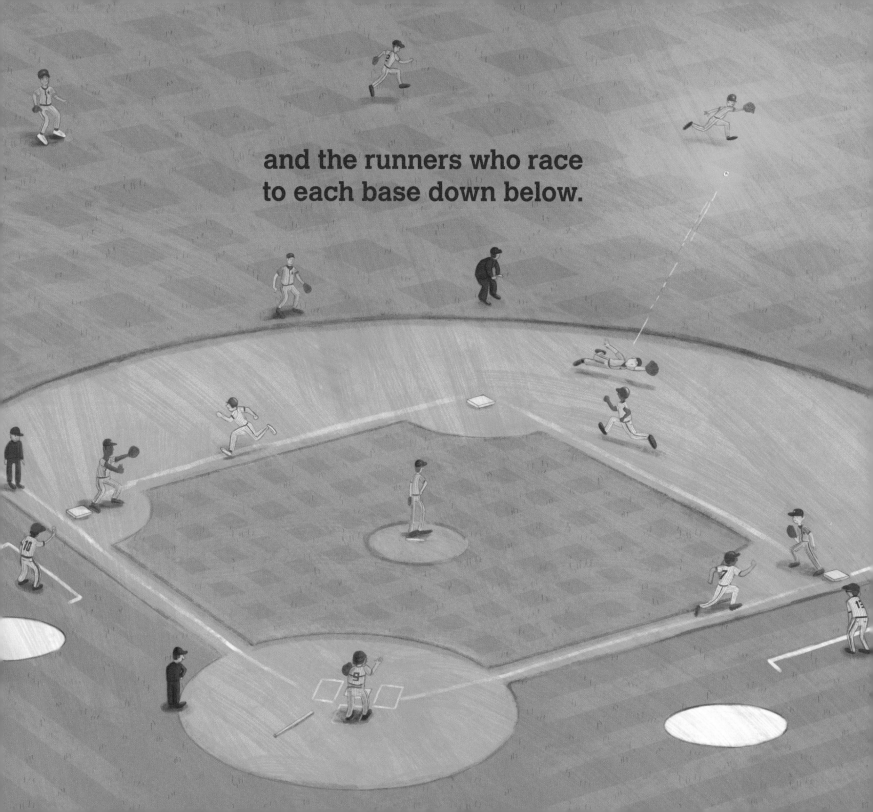

and the runners who race
to each base down below.

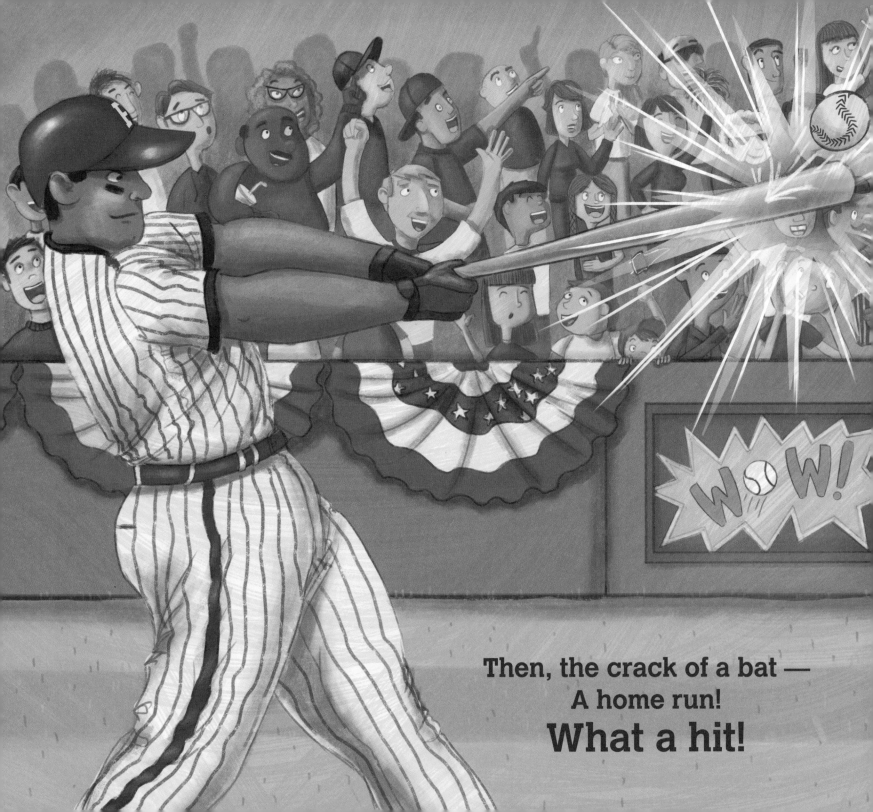

Then, the crack of a bat —
A home run!
What a hit!

Look! The little ball lands in one lucky fan's mitt!

The fans stand and stretch at the late seventh inning.

And the game goes
on, the home team
close to winning.

Everyone cheers. The home team won!

Now the fans are all chanting,

"We're number one!"

Then the crowd waves goodbye.

Goodnight, teams.

You played a great game!
Now sleep well, and sweet dreams.

Goodnight, diamond.

Goodnight, grass.

Goodnight, home plate
where each runner ran past.

Goodnight, bat.

GO RO

Goodnight, mitt

that reached up high and caught a fast hit.

Goodnight, popcorn boxes under the stands.

Goodnight, mascot and goodnight, fans!

Goodnight, friends.

Goodnight,
cars.

Goodnight, stadium, under the stars..

Goodnight,
Daddy.

Goodnight, moon.

Goodnight, baseball,
safe in my room.

To Gene Dahl, a boy's best dad.

Published by
PICTURE WINDOW BOOKS
a Capstone imprint
1710 Roe Crest Drive, North Mankato, Minnesota 56003
www.capstonepub.com

Library of Congress Cataloging-in-Publication data is
available on the Library of Congress website.

ISBN: 978-1-62370-000-3 (hardcover)
ISBN: 978-1-4048-7979-9 (library binding)
ISBN: 978-1-4795-4975-7 (paperback)

Designer: Bob Lentz

Printed in the United States of America in North Mankato, Minnesota.
112017   010926R